Acting Edition

Moonlight Sinatra

by Steven Keyes

|| SAMUEL FRENCH ||

FOR PRODUCTION INQUIRIES

UNITED STATES AND CANADA
info@concordtheatricals.com
1-866-979-0447

UNITED KINGDOM AND EUROPE
licensing@concordtheatricals.co.uk
020-7054-7298

Each title is subject to availability from Concord Theatricals Corp., depending upon country of performance. Please be aware that *MOONLIGHT SINATRA* may not be licensed by Concord Theatricals Corp. in your territory. Professional and amateur producers should contact the nearest Concord Theatricals Corp. office or licensing partner to verify availability.

MOONLIGHT SINATRA was first produced under a different title at the Met Theater, Los Angeles with Rochelle Robinson, Scott Connell, Jon Powell, Steve Keyes, and Leslie Windram in the cast.

A reading of an earlier draft was done at New Dramatists in New York. In the cast were Veronica Cartwright, Bill Cwikowski, Mac Crowell, Steve Keyes, and Jan Leslie Harding.

This version of the play as titled was given a staged reading in Los Angeles with Delaney Driscoll, Jeffrey Johnson, Jon Powell, Colby Rummell, and Jenny Rainwater taking the roles.

The playwright thanks all who contributed to this work.

CHARACTERS

PATSY TYSON – A waitress, mid/late thirties. A "stand-up girl" able to give as good as she gets, but vulnerable and sincere.

ED TYSON – Her husband, late thirties. A "good ole boy" drinker with a short fuse. Misguided; fiercely devoted (in his fashion).

LYNETTE DUFRESNE – A friend, mid-thirties. Chipper, self-involved; a barracuda under the fluff.

DUKE EVANS – Ed's pal, late twenties/early thirties. Sweet; metabolically "slow," not dumb. An innocent.

BOBBY DON "B.D." FLOWERS – From across town, late thirties. Pleasant, sincere (to a fault); romantic but guarded; an aging "dreamboat."

SETTING

A trailer park and surrounding locations
Iota, East Texas

TIME

April

AUTHOR'S NOTE

The play is in two acts.

The dialect written into the text is intended to suggest the language and vernacular of these people and the place. If spoken as written, no attempt at an overly broad Texas "hillbilly" accent should be needed.

For Wynn Handman

ACT I

Scene One

(Ed and Patsy's trailer. 4:00 p.m. **ED** *sits in a lawn chair, center, drinking a beer. There are empty cans lined up on a side table. The scene is cramped and cluttered with half-opened boxes stacked at the upstage wall. The living situation looks very recent and temporary. Water is running from a tap offstage where* **PATSY** *is.)*

ED. Yeah. Things're turnin' aroun'... It's the light at the end of the tunnel... It's always blackest before the sunshine... Ya hear Patsy? Yeah, things're turnin' aroun'. Nothin' like a little adversity to make a man appreciate what he has in life, ya know, Patsy?

> *(He takes an empty chip bag, blows into it and smacks it, making a loud "Pop!")*

PATSY!

PATSY. *(Offstage.)* What?!

ED. I'm jest sayin' about how things're turnin' aroun'... Ya hear what I'm sayin'?

PATSY. *(Offstage.)* Yeah. I'm real glad to hear an' it's about time.

ED. *(Savoring it.)* Assistant Beverage Manager at the Vendome... Ya stay at the table long enough, yer number comes up, right? ...Assistant Beverage Manager at the Vendome.

PATSY. *(Offstage.)* Right Ed, that's real good.

ED. It's a chain.

    *(**PATSY** enters.)*

PATSY. But they didn't hire you yet.

ED. I'm waitin' fer the call.

PATSY. An' yer sure good at waitin'.

ED. What else can I do? You tell me.

PATSY. You could look more.

ED. I been lookin' fer a month. More even...

PATSY. Well, look harder. Get them boots on an' hit the road... That tool 'n' die jest opened.

ED. Ever since them wells was capped there's been nothin'.

PATSY. Oh, Ed yer dreamin'. You never worked on no rig. The rigs pay good money. Roy Hubbard got himself a house an' a boat from what he made roughneckin' on them oil rigs. Started his own business.

ED. A mini-golf hutch.

PATSY. What did ever happen on that job fer him, anyways?

ED. He's had it in fer me ever since high school. Roy Hubbard's had a bug up his butt ever since you ast me to that Sadie Hawkins dance an' he hadda go with Lou Ann Skaggs.

PATSY. He married her. He musta not had too bad a time.

ED. An' you married me.

PATSY. Yeah... Ferget about him.

ED. I said we're gettin' another house. I tole you. *(Beat.)* I'm not workin' with no cracker grease monkeys.

PATSY. Whyn't you try fer somethin' better then? Take a course.

ED. I'm not takin' no courses. I want a position.

PATSY. Looks to me like yer in yer favorite one now. My keys... You seen my keys? At least try to act like yer alive okay, Ed?

ED. Why don't you try actin' like my wife an' give me a little support?

PATSY. I'm runnin' low in the support department, Ed. Real low.

ED. I'm not workin' on no rig.

PATSY. They're gone, Ed. Long gone. They wouldn't hire you anyway. Remember? J.B. tried to set you up down there an' you couldn't get along, as usual.

ED. Well, jest look where it got J.B.

PATSY. We're not talkin' about J.B. so don't get started. You know that gets my back up.

> *(She furiously goes through her bag, then softens and gives* **ED** *a pat on the head.)*

I'm real glad about the Vendome, Ed. Real glad. I hope you get it. Soon. I really hope so.

ED. *(Taking her hand.)* So...?

PATSY. *(Pulls away.)* So, I really hope you become the best assistant beverage manager the Vendome ever had. Manager even. You sure know beverages. Where's my keys?

ED. Goin' down to the diner?

PATSY. No. I got rehearsal. You see my keys? Turn on a light in here. *(She flicks a lamp on and off.)* Is this thing plugged in? Maybe it's the bulb. Ed? Ed?! I need an outlet.

ED. There's one there someplace.

PATSY. Jest don't help me.

ED. I'll help you. *(He points vaguely to a corner.)* There. There's one.

PATSY. That's a phone jack. I need an outlet. I need an outlet. *(She finds a flashlight, snaps it on and off.)* Nothin' in this damn place works includin' you. Help me find my damn keys.

ED. Yer not goin'.

PATSY. In a pig's eye.

ED. *(Takes keys from his shirt pocket and dangles them.)* I said yer not goin' an' yer not goin'.

PATSY. Gimme them keys.

ED. Drop it. I said drop it. Yer not goin'.

PATSY. I'm goin' alright. An' when I get back, I know where you'll be. Right where you are – in that damn chair, passed out, some rerun shinin' in yer face with yer shirt buttons popped –

ED. I'll pop you!

PATSY. Get up an' do it. Do somethin'.

ED. Yer cruisin'.

PATSY. Yer crazy.

> *(She picks up a half-empty beer can and starts pouring the remnants at his feet.)*

ED. You want it? Quit messin' with me. Yer messin' with my mind.

PATSY. Yeah, that's why I'm pourin' it on yer feet.

ED. At least my feet're good fer somethin'.

> *(He kicks at her as she dodges him.)*

PATSY. Goodbye. I'm goin' to rehearse.

ED. Shit!

PATSY. No, shit on you, Ed. Shit on you. I'm doin' everythin' jest like I said. An' I'm not askin' you buddy, I'm tellin' you. I'm goin' to practice my *love scene* in this play with Arthur.

ED. "Arthur"?! Bobby Don Flowers. "Arthur." Hah!

PATSY. Arthur is his confirmation name. He uses it on the stage, yes.

ED. Candy-ass.

PATSY. Now gimme them keys.

ED. *(Stumbling into his boots.)* I'm goin', too. I'm goin' to watch. I wanna see who's tonguin' my wife.

PATSY. Yer disgustin' an' yer not goin'. Gimme them keys.

> *(She lunges at him and he whacks her. She whacks him and they roll around whacking each other.)*

ED. I'll take you fer a ride, honey. *I'll* take you.

PATSY. Lemmego.

> *(She bites **ED**'s hand and grabs the keys as he grabs her ankle, pulling her back.)*

ED. I'm goin' too!

PATSY. On yer rotten mother's grave!

ED. I wanna be with my wife.

PATSY. Yer drunk.

ED. My sweet honeybunch.

PATSY. I'm...GOIN'!

> *(She squirms out of his arms and runs to the door, pitching empty beer cans at him. The phone begins to ring and continues loudly.)*

ED. Shit! Stop! You bitch!

PATSY. You damn party animal!

ED. Ouch! Goddamn!

> *(He falls back.)*

PATSY. Good. Now stay there where you belong.

ED. I'll get you. I'll get you.

PATSY. Too late, Ed honey. You already got me.

> *(She exits.)*

ED. I'll get you.

> *(He crawls back onto the chair, then grabs the remote and turning on a game show,* snaps open a beer and holds it to his head. He finally grabs the phone, which stops ringing just as he picks it up.)*

WHAT?! *(He slams down the receiver, then peers suspiciously at the TV screen.)* Spin you asshole.

> *(Fade to blackout.)*

Scene Two

(Same. The next day. **PATSY** *is sitting painting her toenails. There is classical music on the radio.* Then a knock at the door.)*

PATSY. One sec...

*(***LYNETTE*** *enters.)*

LYNETTE. I jest let myself in, hon.

PATSY. Hey, Lynette.

LYNETTE. I can only stay a minute. Rhonda's out in the car seat. *(She glances around the room.)* The place looks nice. Yer really fixin' it up.

PATSY. Ya like it huh? I'd show ya aroun' but the east wing's bein' redone an' it's a mess.

LYNETTE. So... What happened? How'd the test come out this time? I been on eggs all week... Patsy?

PATSY. We're O-fer-three. Let's jest ferget it.

LYNETTE. Shoot. Okay, well so, Ed's a quart low. Go up to Dallas. See another doctor. There's more than one way to skin a cat. There's modern science. Get another opinion –

PATSY. I think three's the limit. Anyways, I'm up to here with opinions. An' don't even mention the word to Ed. No more doctors. No more tests. That's that.

LYNETTE. That's a shame.

PATSY. Hell, it's jest as well. One baby in this place is enough.

LYNETTE. Poor Ed...

PATSY. Yeah, that's what I mean.

> (**LYNETTE** *stares at a framed picture on the wall.*)

LYNETTE. I love that print. I got some macrame plant hangers I'm not usin' anymore, if you want 'em. Spruce the place up a bit.

PATSY. Sure. Now all I need's some plants... What's up?

LYNETTE. I'm thinkin' about the baby, is all. Ferns give off gas 'er somethin'. I read that. There's a whole oxygen problem in the atmosphere. There's a layer missin'.

PATSY. There's a whole lotta stuff missin' everywhere, Lynette. What's up?

LYNETTE. Well, it's kinda short notice, I know, but I need you to take one a' my shifts this weekend. Or watch the baby.

PATSY. Oh. It's multiple choice.

LYNETTE. No. It's a' emergency. It's J.B.

PATSY. Now what?

LYNETTE. He's got one day out fer good behavior an' I wanna go see him... He's gotta be back Sundy noon. It's a three-hour drive... We jes got one night... He's changed. The freezer has changed him.

PATSY. "Cooler." It's called the "cooler."

LYNETTE. He sounds so different. I could tell jest hearin' his voice. He's been askin' about the baby. He sent her a li'l outfit. Real cute. It's like a jungle suit an' it says "Don't Tread on Me" an' it's got a cute li'l snake 'er somethin' on it... He ast how you an' Ed're doin' –

PATSY. That's real nice a' him.

LYNETTE. You bein' the godparents an' all. He says he's been goin' to the chapel there an' he's real close with the pastor an' in therapy groups an' he's real sorry about the house 'n' all... He's not drinkin' anymore an' wants to set things right when he gets out.

PATSY. He's gonna build us a new one, huh? Well, tell him to add on a deck this time. Damn Lynette. "No casa. Comprehende?" That house was all we had left from Momma an' Daddy an' fool J.B. goes on a bender an' burns the thing to the ground cuz he's spooked.

LYNETTE. He was confused. Them blacks moved in right behind y'all an' he got mixed up. He burnt the wrong house. Thank God nobody got hurt... I don't say it was right but you both have them same awnings.

PATSY. *Had* them same awnings.

LYNETTE. Patsy, I realize you lost yer house. I realize that.

PATSY. And?

LYNETTE. I know it's been hard on you both. I said we'd make it up to you. What else can I say?

PATSY. Goodbye. I gotta get goin'. Call Bonnie.

LYNETTE. Her momma's got the upchucks.

PATSY. I'm sorry, but maybe it's a sign. All fer the best. God don't want you goin' to see J.B. God has good sense. He knows when to let sleepin' dogs lie.

LYNETTE. I don't know... The whole thing's Ed's fault anyways.

PATSY. Excuse me?

LYNETTE. I'm sayin' Ed shouldn't a' left J.B. that night.

PATSY. Ed ain't J.B.'s babysitter.

LYNETTE. Runnin' off after you an' mad too, he was. An' now you an' Bobby Don Flowers goin' hot an' heavy at them rehearsals, so I hear.

PATSY. Yeah? Well, we're runnin' off to Acapulco next week so excuse me while I pack –

LYNETTE. I'm jest tellin' you what I hear is all. The green-eyed monster strikes with a powerful venom an' as a friend I'm tellin' you, no man's gonna stand fer that kinda monkey business goin' on right under his nose. You know how Ed is.

PATSY. Do I ever, an' the day Ed does somethin' that ain't operated by remote control from that chair is the day I drop over in amazement. An' I got play rehearsal so...

(**PATSY** *gathers her bag.*)

LYNETTE. Play 'er no play. "The heart has its reasons that reason knows nothin' about."

PATSY. Knit it in a sampler. Come on, I think I hear the baby cryin'.

(*As they exit,* **DUKE** *appears at the screen door.*)

LYNETTE. Oh, my lord!

DUKE. Hey, Lynette.

LYNETTE. Duke Wayne Evans, you scared the livin' tar outta me.

DUKE. Okay then... Hey, Patsy.

PATSY. Hey Duke. Ed ain't here an' we're on our way out.

LYNETTE. Duke, you know my baby Rhonda?

DUKE. I know that's her name.

LYNETTE. I know yer good with children.

PATSY. Lynette, we gotta go.

LYNETTE. I got no rush. How's yer momma, Duke?

DUKE. You know. The same.

PATSY. Well, it's my house an' I say we gotta go. He can't watch yer baby, Lynette.

DUKE. Can I wait here fer Ed? (*He sits.*)

LYNETTE. I'm sure Duke is responsible.

PATSY. Let's go!

LYNETTE. Jest hold on a minute, Patsy. You let Duke speak fer himself.

> (**DUKE** *is at the table munching from a cereal box.*)

Duke, you wanna make a couple bucks?

DUKE. No. I can't watch no baby.

PATSY. I don't know when Ed'll be back.

LYNETTE. That's not very neighborly, Duke.

DUKE. So, I'll jes wait here fer him.

PATSY. Get in line, buddy. I been waitin' fer years.

LYNETTE. Don't mind me!

PATSY. Okay Duke. But lock up if you leave and don't re-program the damn TV. You know how Ed hates that.

DUKE. No problemo.

LYNETTE. Yeah, right!

> (**LYNETTE** *stalks out the door followed by* **PATSY. DUKE** *sits munching on cereal and channel surfing. There is a lull in the action, then we see* **ED**'s *head pop up in the window behind.*)

ED. Pssst! Psst! Hey, boy!

DUKE. What? ...Ed?! What are you doin' out there?

ED. What're you doin' *in* there?

DUKE. Waitin' fer you.

> (**ED** *rushes in through the door.*)

ED. Well, it's yer lucky day cuz here I am!

DUKE. Ain't you workin' yet?

ED. Yeah, I'm workin' on a' idea. Turn that TV off an' listen to me. *(He grabs and clicks off the remote.)* Where'd Patsy go?

DUKE. I dunno.

ED. I do.

DUKE. Then why'd you ask?

ED. Boy, lemme have a talk with you. Yer my pal, my buddy, right? We go way back. How long has it been?

> *(**DUKE** counts to himself.)*

I was the first one at yer door when y'all moved here, as I recall.

DUKE. You needed a jump on yer car.

ED. Yeah. I got you that job at the bowlin' alley, right? ... So, you got fired fer jammin' the snack machine...

DUKE. You said it'd take slugs.

ED. The point is, I been there fer you –

DUKE. I don't got any money, Ed.

ED. Huh! You think that's what I want? Money? That's all you thinka me? *(Re: cereal box.)* Oh, an' lookee here: you could get yer own Secret Decoder Map fer three easy box tops. Is that what yer savin' fer? Tsk, tsk. A smart boy like you readin' cereal boxes. Tsk, tsk.

DUKE. Leave me be.

ED. Boy, this is a new Ed yer lookin' at. This is the new me. I'm a changed man.

DUKE. Uh-huh. Yer wearin' a tie.

ED. Stop starin'! These here is my lookin'-fer-work clothes. *(Beat.)* Listen to me, boy: things've been rough lately. I been low. Real low. But today, my friend, all that changed. I went across town to the parish there an' spoke to the father – you know, in private-like an' I am tellin' you, praise the lord. I have found my way! I went into the confession there an' I got down on my knees. I kneeled down an' I sweated an' I strained... I'm jest glad I don't have more sins – my knees couldn't take it. So, I said my peace an' then it came to me, like a vision. I knew what I was missin'. An' what do you think that was? What?

DUKE. A cushion.

ED. Faith! FAITH! I had lost my faith – but I jes got it back an' I have faith that you are gonna come through fer me... I'd do it myself but it has to be *in-cog-nito*. That's what I need you fer... All you havta do is join up in that play they're doin' down there at the center.

DUKE. Play?

ED. Yeah. I want you to be my plant. I heard it on the news. You "plant" someone someplace where you gotta know what's goin' on. Like governments do an' corporations. Then the plant like they call 'em, tells what he sees.

DUKE. I can't be in no play. No way.

ED. Come on. You jes gotta join up. Jes go an' spy.

DUKE. Spy? On who?

ED. Patsy.

DUKE. Patsy? She's in that play there? What the heck's she doin' that you wanna spy on her fer? I like her. She gives Momma her shots. No. I'm not gonna be planted by you 'er nobody else to spy on her. She's fun. I like her.

ED. She's *fun*. She's fun, alright. She's so much fun she's got extra fun an' she's givin' it to Bobby Don Flowers.

DUKE. Who's Bobby Don Flowers?

ED. This joker from crosstown. Plays organ fer the Sundy services. Wears bow ties. He come into the diner. I know. Lynette seen him. First, he starts in on Patsy, then she starts takin' her break with him. In a booth. An' then she's givin' him pie. On the house. An' now he's got her in some freak show an' they're goin' at it behind my back.

DUKE. I don't know 'im.

ED. You will.

DUKE. I ain't no actor.

ED. This is yer big chance. Get you outta the house. Away from yer momma an' Sissy an' into the big time. You ain't spooked are ya?

DUKE. No. I'm jes thinkin'. What kinda *play* is it? I won't do nudity.

ED. Take yer mind outta the trash. It's jes fer make-believe. Scary but fake scary. Like *Halloween* 'er *The Wolfman*. Witches an' the like, I hear tell... People changin' into animals an' flyin' away... It'll be fun. *(Beat.)* Well? I need an experienced man fer this job. I'll give you that fire hat I got. Fer yer collection.

DUKE. The one with the badge?

ED. Uh-huh.

DUKE. An' all I gotta do is tell you if I see Patsy an' this guy gettin' together?

ED. Uh-huh.

DUKE. *(A beat; he thinks...)* Okay. But I want the hat now, though.

ED. It's yers, buddy. An' I'll even throw in some box tops.
Yer jest savin' my honeybunch fer her big boy where
she belongs, that's what yer doin', uh-huh.

DUKE. Uh-huh.

> (**ED** *throws his arm over* **DUKE***'s shoulder.*
> *Blackout.*)

Scene Three

(The bare stage of the "Town Center," a renovated barn. **BOBBY DON "B.D." FLOWERS** *sits with a towel draped over his shoulders.* **PATSY** *stands behind him, cutting his hair.)*

PATSY. I think it's jest wonderful, you playin' at them Sundy services. *(Beat.)* They say to give service is to show God's love.

B.D. I think it's important to be involved.

PATSY. Put yer head down. *(Beat.)* I admire musical ability. My daddy was musical, too. He was a performer. A singer. An' a mailman.

B.D. A singin' mailman.

PATSY. He never made much of a livin' singin' but the dogs on his route never gave him any trouble.

B.D. That must be where you get your talent.

PATSY. You think? You do? Thank you. I respect that comin' from you, I really do. I wish Momma could hear you say that.

B.D. Your momma was a singer, too?

PATSY. Momma? Lord no, Daddy was the one. When he wasn't juiced. He was a drunk alright, there I said it. But – oh lord, was he fun at parties! Jest a beautiful voice. Momma married him fer it. She used to say, "If he'd only stop talkin' an' sing!" *(B.D. flinches.)* Oops, sorry. Almost took yer ear off. There I go – goin' on, jes like my daddy. Big mouth me.

B.D. I like to hear you talk. You're astute.

PATSY. Well, sir, I been called a lotsa things but that is the first time I been called a *stute*. What's a "stute"? That's French, it'n it?

B.D. ...Yes. It means "observant...intelligent. Artful."

PATSY. Well, yer jest a walkin' dictionary. An' you know French. I think that's great. I love languages. I took a course once down at the community college in "Romance Languages" but they fired the teacher fer knockin' up the office girl. *(She brushes his shoulders.)* Well, that's that. An' you sir, are done.

    (She sits.)

B.D. And I thank you, ma'am.

PATSY. An' I'd say wait till you count yer ears 'fore you say that.

B.D. Ed's a lucky guy.

PATSY. Yer jes too nice an' I think Ed's luck has jest about run out.

B.D. You mean his job and everything...

PATSY. Yeah. *An' everythin'...* I tell you, if it keeps up, Ed's gonna need bloodhounds to find a job. I jest don't know... Somethin' happened... You shoulda seen him when we first met. It was a dance Halloween night. Me an' Lynette was dressed up like the Doublemint Twins. We don't look nothin' alike but when she wore heels an' I wore flats we was about the same height with wigs. Anyways, we're standin' there next to the punchbowl an' Ed comes up an' he's wearin' a Dracula costume – this cape an' everythin' – silk, an' he says – jest asks me flat out if he can bite my neck. He had on them plastic fangs an' he opened his mouth, sorta hissin'. *(She imitates this.)* He said he needed to practice cuz he was helpin' with the blood drive down at the firehouse... He was bein' funny an' I sure thought he was. I laughed an' then we danced – he's a good dancer – then after, when we went out to the car it was rainin' an' he put his cape down. He jest laid it right down in the mud an' walked me to the car. His momma never fergave him fer ruinin' that cape she made by stickin' it in the mud fer me. *(Beat.)* Hell, that was a lotta talk an' about 2,000 beers ago. Now Ed jest wears me out...

We still got that same damn car an' he still thinks he's funny but I don't laugh much anymore. Too much talk. That's a big problem with Mister Ed. He jest can't stop talkin'. But yer nice and polite. I like that in a man.

B.D. I can talk a blue streak when I want.

PATSY. You never been married, right?

B.D. No.

PATSY. You don't wanna talk about it.

B.D. Let's just say Iota's not the place for me.

PATSY. An' may I be so "astute" as to imply where the place fer you might be? *(No response.)* You ever been to New York City? That's the Big Time, right? Like the song says: "New York, New York"...

B.D. I was there once. When I was twelve. Haven't been back since. *(Beat.)* I was on TV.

PATSY. No?!

B.D. Yes.

PATSY. Well, the "Mystery Guest" has been holdin' out on us. You been on TV.

B.D. Once. When I was twelve.

PATSY. That's one more time than anybody else I know, present company included. What'd you do?

B.D. I sang an' played piano... It was one of those contest shows called *Big Tiny Talents*. My uncle was the host.

PATSY. Oh. Despotism.

B.D. No. I had to try out. I played and sang to "Swingin' on a Star." I wanted to do a medley but they had a time limit.

PATSY. I know that one. That's a good one.

B.D. Not good enough.

PATSY. I'm sure you were great.

B.D. Well, I kept playing. I *played* that song. All four verses. My uncle said, "You didn't play good Bobby, but you played loud." So...

PATSY. So, you won.

B.D. No. But I like to think I've improved...

PATSY. An' that's all that matters, what yer doin' now. You gotta use everythin' you got in this world. That's a very special talent. *(Beat.)* An' that haircut is fine, if I do say so myself. It'll grow out nice fer the play. I have to say: you are the best-lookin' witch-boy I ever seen.

B.D. You like actin' in this play, Patsy?

PATSY. Well, I love gettin' to wear that red dress, that's fersure. An' I love what yer doin' with yer role in the play. You sir, are a true actor. Yer good enough to go to England. That's where all the real actors go, right? Except Lucy. Miss Lucille Ball, thank you very much. She was a waitress, too. An' a chorus girl. An' a model. An' lotsa things before. I modeled fer a while. Different parts, you know – hands, eyes. Momma used to ask when were we ever gonna see my whole face.

I said, "They don't pay to see my face, they pay fer my toenails." Then she'd say I had the biggest feet on a girl she'd ever seen an' they must be crazier than me to pay fer 'em. *(Beat.)* God love, I miss her. She passed. She's gone.

B.D. I'm sorry. My momma's gone, too. A year come June.

PATSY. Well, we're jest a coupla orphans it'n we? I'll tell you, I was a mess. I cried and cried. "Waaah!" I wanted to cry jes like Lucy does when Ricky yells at her but we was in the funeral home an' everybody was lookin' so serious. But I swear I almost did...

B.D. *(After a beat.)* You are a charmin' woman.

PATSY. Get out.

B.D. It's true. When you're just sittin' here talking, being yourself, you are a charmin' woman.

PATSY. Shoot. I'll cut yer hair till yer bald fer sayin' that! "Charmin'"... Yer pretty darn charmin' yerself.

> *(There is a clap of thunder. She shudders.)*

That gave me a fright... It's light out, jes after noon... "April showers bring May flowers."

B.D. My grandad used to say, "Every time it rains, it rains pennies from Heaven."

PATSY. I think that's a song.

B.D. I was five. I didn't know it at the time.

> *(Beat.)*

PATSY. It's stoppin' jest as quick as it started.

B.D. *(Digs in his pocket.)* Here.

PATSY. A penny.

B.D. I think this is *the* penny. The very penny. The penny from Heaven.

> *(He gently puts the penny into her hand.)*

PATSY. You sure are funny, Mr. Bobby Don Flowers. You are about the funniest, sweetest man I ever met.

> *(There is another faint roll of thunder. Blackout.)*

Scene Four

(**LYNETTE** *is on the phone.*)

LYNETTE. Could you, Bonnie? Oh, that'd be such a big help. She's jest a li'l angel an' won't be any trouble. Thanks hon, yer a life saver. Li'l Rhonda jest loves her Aunt Bonnie to pieces. She's sendin' you some sugar right through this here phone... (*Beat.*) Shoot, I'm fine. You know, still down at *The Greenhouse*. Pullin' extra shifts...

"No rest fer the wicked," as they say... (*Beat.*)

Patsy? Uh-huh, she's still there. Sorta... (*Beat.*)

You mean you haven't heard? (*Beat.*)

Well, she's – she's, let's say, got another pot on the stove...

Uh-huh, an' I tell you, Ed is fit to be tied. It is jest tearin' him up. An' I can't say as I blame him. Losin' his house an' his job an' now this. It was a freak accident, the house burnin' but I won't go into it an' then you know the ambulance service let him go cuz a' his drinkin'. I like Ed but I have to say, I wouldn't want him drivin' if I was losin' blood... (*Beat.*)

I've tried to warn her as a friend, but she's carryin' on with that drama troupe down at the center an' decided she's the star attraction of Iota. Queen a' the Lone Star State!... (*Beat.*)

Bobby Don Flowers...from the subdivision over near Singin' Hills. He's strange. Quiet type, *you know*. "Still water runs deep," right? *I* wouldn't trust him. An' now she's on this kick an' they're doin' this play an' she don't have time fer nothin'! My baby could be crawlin' the streets an' would she lift a finger to help? N-O. No good's gonna come of this, that's all I can say an' I tell you, she'll fall. Hard. But you know me, hon – I don't like to judge... (*Beat.*)

Uh-huh. I'll drop the baby off about noon. I'll put in a extra bottle an' her tummy medicine. Oh, an' Bonnie – she loves the stories, so jes prop her up in fronta the tube an' she won't make a teeny tiny peep. *(Suddenly, there is the loud, piercing cry of a baby.)* Oh! There she goes – that's jes her, hon – she wants her momma. *(She hangs up, then yells off.)* Okay! I'm comin'!

(Blackout.)

Scene Five

(One week later. Basement of the Town Center. **DUKE** *sits eating a bag lunch.* **ED** *enters, sneaks up from behind, grabs a banana from the lunch, and with a "fast draw," aims at* **DUKE**.*)*

ED. Go ahead, make my day!

DUKE. What are you doin' here, Ed?! They're gonna see you. Why're you here?!

ED. You ask too many questions.

(He "shoots" **DUKE** *with the banana.)*

I jest stopped by to check on yer activities – "agent."

DUKE. Quit yer foolin' an' leave me be. I'm doin' this like you ast but I ain't no actor.

ED. You did that Christmas show two years in a row. You were good. Played a sheep as I recall –

DUKE. I was a goat. They had too many sheep so I hadda be a goat –

ED. An' now yer a spy. That's a step up, I'd say.

DUKE. I still don't get why you want me to spy on her fer. I like Patsy.

ED. What's she been sayin' to you?

DUKE. She ain't been sayin' nothin'.

ED. ...*Tell me.* What're they doin'?

DUKE. Nothin'. They're jest actin' like they do.

ED. Actin' my butt!

(Noises offstage.)

DUKE. See there now, somebody's comin'! Go on, get out. Hide.

(ED scrambles around and then exits to the kitchen, left. PATSY enters, right. DUKE sits and continues eating furiously.)

PATSY. Duke!

DUKE. What?!

PATSY. Yer here early.

DUKE. I like to...have time to...prepare.

PATSY. Yer dedicated. I didn't know you were a thespian.

(DUKE peers at her suspiciously.)

That's an actor. Someone who performs. It's Latin. 'Er Greek. 'Er I don't know. We'll ask Arthur when he comes. *(Beat.)* You know Duke, I was surprised when you showed up here last week. I never took you fer the type. Yer always so quiet when I'm over at the house.

DUKE. Momma can't stand too much noise. If too much is goin' on she gets cramps.

PATSY. I'm glad Sissy's able to give yer momma her shots now. Me bein' so busy an' all. I hope she starts feelin' better.

DUKE. She's at the mall today. They got a' elephant sale there. She's shoppin'.

PATSY. Shoppin's good medicine. *White* elephant. Yer momma's at a *white* elephant sale. That's a sorta gag name they give to everythin' they can't sell. To get rid of it.

DUKE. Oh. *(He offers her an apple.)* You want one? I didn't bite it.

PATSY. No, thanks. I gotta change. Arthur'll be here any minute.

DUKE. Who's Arthur?

PATSY. You know. Bobby Don. He plays John, the witch-boy.

DUKE. Oh, the big fella with the belt buckle. That's some piece 'a hardware. I like them masks he's got on there.

PATSY. Those are the masks of comedy an' drama. That's the emblem fer actin'. They presented that to him last year when he played Hamlet.

DUKE. I don't know that one.

PATSY. It's jest the biggest part ever written in the theatre. *(She pronounces it "thee-aye-tur.")* And Arthur played it. They did the short version but it was still pretty long... That's the first time I seen him onstage. He sure was somethin'. Dyed his hair an' everythin'. Arthur is dedicated.

DUKE. Sissy dyes her hair.

PATSY. Arthur is an artist.

DUKE. Arthur?

PATSY. I said. Bobby Don. Arthur is his stage name.

DUKE. Will I get a stage name?

PATSY. If you want. But don't use Arthur. That's taken.

(**DUKE** *offers her a snack cake.*)

DUKE. Want a Ding-Dong?

PATSY. No thanks. I gotta keep in shape. That costume they got me in don't leave no room fer Ding-Dongs.

DUKE. Pretty sexy, huh? I bet Ed's gonna like that.

PATSY. *Ed.* Ed got his chance. But this is the theatre. Ed don't go fer show business. He likes to make a scene but he don't like the theatre. *(Beat.)* Now, I gotta change my skirt real quick. Arthur oughta be here any minute.

DUKE. Can I watch y'all rehearse?

PATSY. We're runnin' past our scene, Duke. Jes me an' Arthur. We ain't doin' yer section yet.

DUKE. Well…I can watch you guys practice. I like that scene in the forest.

PATSY. You stay down here an' keep a look-out, okay? An' make sure to dump that trash when yer done 'er Mavis will rag us all week about the bugs…

> *(She exits left to the kitchen.* **DUKE** *jumps up and runs to the kitchen door. There is a long beat as* **DUKE** *listens at the door, eating the banana, then* **PATSY** *re-enters, knocking* **DUKE** *aside.)*

Goldarn Duke, what're you doin' there? Keep outta the way 'fore you get yer head knocked off. *(Beat.)* Now, you stay here like I said an' wait on Arthur. You tell him I'm upstairs.

> *(She exits right.* **DUKE** *waits a moment, then calls through the kitchen door.)*

DUKE. Ed? Ed. Come on out, she's gone. The coast is clear. Ed?

> *(***ED*** *re-enters, hunched over in pain.)*

That was a close call. She didn't see you, right? I thought fer sure she was gonna spot you in there. Where'd you hide?

ED. Under the sink.

DUKE. Shoot, I hope yer not lookin' fer a plumber job.

> *(There are footsteps offstage.)*

Go on now, there's somebody else comin'… You better get outta here.

ED. That him?

DUKE. Who?

ED. That fool. That "witch-boy."

DUKE. Don't you start nothin'.

ED. I won't start nothin'. Yet... I wanna be good 'n' ready fer him...

DUKE. Go on now. Get out.

> (**ED** *rushes back into the kitchen.* **DUKE** *follows behind and puts his ear to the door.* **B.D.** *enters.*)

B.D. Hey, Duke. What're you up to?

DUKE. Nothin'!

B.D. What's goin' on in the kitchen?

DUKE. Nothin'!

B.D. That sounds like a whole lotta nothin'. *(Beat.)* Patsy here?

DUKE. She's upstairs waitin' on you. So, let's get on up there.

> (**DUKE** *crosses to the outer door.* **B.D.** *stops him.*)

B.D. You been workin' on your dance, Duke?

DUKE. Yeah...

B.D. Let's see some of it... Do your chant.

DUKE. It ain't done though... I can't get riled up, I jes ate.

B.D. Practice makes perfect, Duke. Come on, I'll do it with you.

(Begins to recite.) "A witch-boy from the mountain came –"

DUKE. *(Hesitates a beat.)* "A witch-boy from the mountain came –"

B.D. "A pinin' to be human –"

DUKE. A pinin' to be human –"

(**DUKE** *closes his eyes, begins to sway.*)

B.D. & DUKE. "Fer he had seen the fairest gal,

A gal named Barbara Allen –"

(**B.D.** *slowly backs out the door, exits.*)

DUKE. "O, Conjur man, O, Conjur man,

Please do this thing I'm wantin' –

Please change me to a –"

(**DUKE** *opens his eyes as* **ED** *appears in front of him. Fade out.*)

Scene Six

(Continuous. Upstairs onstage, the Town Center. We see the beginnings of a set: cardboard cut-out trees and green tinsel "moss" hanging from the ceiling.)

B.D. That's some dress.

PATSY. I wore my long skirt. To get a feel –

B.D. – For the character.

PATSY. Right. I'm a regular glamor girl, huh?

B.D. Always a *woman*... "Cherchez la femme."

PATSY. Okay. There you go with that French again. I love when you talk like that. I don't know what the heck it means but I sure do love it. *(Beat.)* Jest look how they fixed this place up with new hangin' lights 'n' everythin'... It's excitin'. I'm really likin' Howard, too. He's a good director. First, I didn't think he liked me but now I feel real good about everythin'.

B.D. Good.

PATSY. *(After a beat.)* Do you believe in dreams? This gal down at the diner says dreams're the door to yer unconscious.

B.D. I believe that.

PATSY. You do? I knew you would. *(Beat.)* I had the craziest dream last night. Jest crazy...

B.D. Was it a good dream?

PATSY. It was late, real dark. I was in my car on the highway an' it jes wouldn't move. I wasn't on empty, I had a full tank. All the other cars were speedin' along, passin' me up but that damn car jest wouldn't start. I don't even know what stopped it. It jest stopped.

B.D. Did you go for help?

PATSY. Uh-huh. Yep, I got outta the car an' waved but nobody stopped. I could feel the wind on my face. "Whoosh." All the other cars were goin' by faster'n before. It was like I was standing there fer hours – then one car stopped. This is the funny part...this probably sounds crazy but when this one car stopped on the other side of the road, you was inside.

B.D. Dreams can tell you a lot. I've been having all kinds of dreams too, lately. I think this play must be workin' its spell on us.

PATSY. You know, that must be it.

B.D. It helps to get a feel for the play... Patsy, I want to do something before the others get here. Improvisation.

PATSY. Uh-huh. Great. What's that?

B.D. That's when you don't know what you're doin'...but you do it anyway. It's a technique. You don't use the words, you just do what you feel.

PATSY. *(Closing her eyes.)* Uh-huh...

B.D. But you have to keep your eyes open. I'll start. Now you go off and come back on and I'll be choppin' wood.

> (**PATSY** *walks off, and* **B.D.** *begins to mime chopping wood. She slinks back on and stands mute with her arms outstretched.)*

"Barbara!"

> *(No response.)*

"Barbara!"

> *(No response.)*

Patsy –

PATSY. We're not supposed to use words.

B.D. Not the words in the play. Your own words. Make 'em up.

PATSY. Oh. Dumbo me.

B.D. So, you go off.

(She exits, then re-enters.)

PATSY. "John! John! What are you doin' there?"

B.D. "I'm choppin' wood fer the long winter ahead."

PATSY. "You look so hot and tired in that shirt. Why don't you take it off?"

B.D. "I'm fine, thanks. Yer momma came by today –"

PATSY. "Oh? How is she?"

(She mimes helping him stack "logs.")

B.D. "She came by to say that she don't want me around you no more. She says I have to leave –"

PATSY. "Oh! She don't mean that! She's been sick."

B.D. "– But I won't!"

PATSY. "You can't! You jest can't!"

(She throws herself on him.)

"I don't know what I'd do if you left! I might do somethin' crazy! Now take off this hot, sweaty shirt an' I'll throw it in the wash!"

*(She pushes **B.D.** back and crawls on top of him.)*

B.D. "Barbara, the logs! –" Patsy! What are you doin'?

PATSY. Improvisin' – "John."

(She kisses him.)

B.D. Patsy!

(She kisses him again.)

PATSY. "John!"

B.D. "Barbara!"

(He grabs and kisses her.)

What am I doin'?

PATSY. Yer doin' fine.

(She kisses him again.)

B.D. Just fine?

(He kisses her again.)

PATSY. More than fine.

B.D. What about Ed?

PATSY. "Sher shay la fem!"

*(They roll on the floor, kissing in a wild embrace. The cardboard trees shudder behind them as one slowly falls, revealing **DUKE**, who stares down at them then runs off. Blackout.)*

Scene Seven

(Two nights later. PATSY *and* ED *are in the car.* ED *is driving and brooding, sucking his teeth.* PATSY *is compulsively changing the radio dial, creating white noise and static.)*

PATSY. I can't never find that damn station when I need to.

ED. Which?

PATSY. That one from Baton Rouge. Classical.

ED. *Oh.* "Classical"... Jest pick a station an' leave it. Quit that switchin'.

PATSY. Well, why don't *you* quit suckin' yer teeth? You know I hate that.

ED. I ain't suckin' my teeth.

(PATSY *imitates him loudly.)*

Well, then gimme a toothpick. You know I get food up in there. Gimme a toothpick.

PATSY. I don't have a damn toothpick. An' if you'd give me the damn car you could stay home an' pick yer teeth till they fall outta yer head.

ED. I tole you. I got bowlin' an' I'm not waitin' on you to pick me up.

PATSY. No, I wait on you, that's it. Right. I could get kilt 'er God-knows-what in that parkin' lot waitin' fer you an' that damn bowlin' team.

ED. Why don't *he* drive you home?

PATSY. Who's *he?*

ED. *Him.*

PATSY. If it's Arthur you mean, *he* can't rehearse tonight. *He* won't be there.

ED. Where's *he* gonna be?

PATSY. Not that it's any a' yer business but he happens to be judgin' in the speech an' drama contest down at the high school. Then next week is the art fair, fer yer information. He's a judge there, too... Arthur is an artist.

> (**ED** *chuckles cynically.*)

ED. Bullshit artist.

PATSY. Well, you'd sure know all about that.

> (*They sit silent for a beat.*)

Maybe yer friend Duke could gimme a ride home on the backa his little two-wheeler. He's a sweet guy, kinda slow... I don't know why the hell he's in the show. I mean them Christmas pageants are one thing – playin' a sheep –

ED. He was a goat.

PATSY. Goat. But he pops up an' there ain't enough men as it is – jest like in real life. So, now he's playin' four different parts an' I'll be surprised if he can learn the lines. There's one scene – oh, it's so funny – he's gotta do this little dance an' cast a spell over us an' well – I'm jest glad we got two more weeks cuz right now he looks like a duck in heat.

ED. He's good at animals.

PATSY. Well, he sure can't dance.

ED. I should play that part.

PATSY. You were a fine dancer Ed, I'll give you that.

ED. Whaddaya mean "were"? (*Beat.*) Remember that Halloween. That school dance when we met? ...We hit it off right away. Yer legs jes wouldn't quit.

PATSY. Yeah, so? *(She fiddles with the radio dial.)* This damn reception...

> *(***ED** starts to hum.)*

ED. Moonlight Sinatra.

PATSY. What?

ED. *Our song.* "Moonlight Sinatra." At that Halloween dance. I gave the band five extra bucks jest to play it twice.

PATSY. Oh, fer heaven's sake, Ed. That's not the name of it. It's called "Moonlight *Sonata.*" An' it's not a song. Wrong as usual. It's a classical piece. You play it on the piano.

ED. That's where I got the idea. The other one. I seen them commercials. You know, the ones fer them music collections. All that fancy "classical," like you call it. I was sittin' there one day an' it came to me... So, I called it "Moonlight Sinatra." He's our fav'rite. He did it "his way"...

PATSY. He was *yer* fav'rite...

ED. Yeah, that's what I said – *our* fav'rite. They called him "Chairman of the Board."

PATSY. That's you alright: Chairman of the B-O-R-E-D.

> *(***ED** scowls and takes a beat.)*

ED. Fly me to the moon.

PATSY. Well, don't ferget to write.

ED. The name a' our song. Remember? I made it up. *Fer us.* That's what I called it. "Moonlight Sinatra"... Fly-me-to-the-moon... You know the rest. *(Beat.)* Sing it.

PATSY. That's all in the past. I'm not singin' in the damn car. An' watch the road, yer weavin'.

ED. "Fly Me to the Moon." *Our song.* I want you to sing it.

PATSY. Oh, Ed...

ED. Sing it.

> *(He slams on the brakes, veering the car to a rough stop.)*

Sing it!

PATSY. You maniac!

ED. You know it. Sing it!

PATSY. Let me outta this car! Lemme out! Kill yerself if you want but yer not takin' me with you. Yer a maniac an' I'm sicka you.

ED. *(Wailing.)* Fly me to the moon! *Sing it!* Fly me to the moon! Fly me to the moon!

PATSY. You can go to the moon an' stay there fer all the hell I care, you damn deadbeat!

> *(She gets out of the car and runs off.)*

ED. *(Screaming after her.)* You know it! Sing it! SING IT! SING IIIIITT!

> *(After this tirade, he slumps down into the driver's seat, his head on the steering wheel and hums, trailing off into an unintelligible whimper. Fade out.)*

ACT II

Scene One

(One week later. Lynette's house. After dark. We see a shadowy figure peering into the kitchen window. LYNETTE is half-asleep, her head on the table. There is a knocking at the door.)

LYNETTE. Shhh! Who the heck's –

ED. *(Offstage.)* Lynette, open up. Lemme in.

(She picks up a small axe.)

LYNETTE. Who's that? Who's there?

ED. *(Offstage.)* It's me. Open up.

LYNETTE. Who's me?

ED. *(Offstage.)* Me. Ed.

LYNETTE. Ed? Is that you?

ED. *(Offstage.)* Yeah. Lemme in.

LYNETTE. How do I know? Say somethin' else.

ED. *(Offstage.)* When J.B. gets outta jail, I'm gonna bust what's left a' his ass fer burnin' down our house.

LYNETTE. Ed.

(She quickly clicks the locks and opens the door. ED rushes into the room, disheveled and covered in leaves and mud.)

LYNETTE. Ed. My lord, where you been? They been lookin'
all over fer you. Where you been? You look like a wild
man. Yer a mess...

ED. Don't you say nothin' about this. Don't say a word.
Drop that. *(Beat.)* You sleep with an axe?

LYNETTE. I'm alone with a baby in the other room that I
jest got to sleep, thank you very much.

ED. Don't you say you saw me.

LYNETTE. They got everybody lookin' fer you. *(She hands
him a newspaper.)* That's a good picture, too. Where you
been stayin'? What're you doin'? What're you gonna do?

ED. I been makin' plans... *(Staring at the newspaper.)*
Dopes. I'll show them... *(He cackles fiendishly.)*

LYNETTE. Shhh. You'll wake the baby. Her colic's been
actin' up and I jest got her to sleep.

ED. *(Mocking her.)* "You'll wake the baby." You gotta beer?

     (He sits heavily.)

LYNETTE. No. An' it's after midnight. The Quik Mart is closed.

ED. So, Patsy's been wonderin' where I am. They all been
wonderin' –

     *(He grabs baby bottle off the table and takes
     a long swig.)*

LYNETTE. I don't know that she's been thinkin' too much
about it –

ED. I hope she thinks I'm dead, too.

LYNETTE. She's gettin' ready fer her play...

ED. "Her play..."

LYNETTE. She ain't even been at the diner in almost a
week. She ast fer the time off.

ED. She's not workin'? Is lover boy Frutti-Tutti keepin' her in diamonds now? He don't even like girls. Homo jerkoff.

LYNETTE. Well, then he's a better actor then we all think. He's doin' a good job on Patsy.

ED. What?!

LYNETTE. Shhh... You'll wake the baby.

> *(She stands behind him, stroking his head and picking stray leaves out of his hair.)*

I know what you need... Take a shower an' cool off, Ed. Simmer down. Stay here if you want. I won't tell. Give you one a' J.B.'s clean shirts.

ED. When's he gettin' out anyway?

LYNETTE. Who knows? Six months. Three if he's good. I been so lonely here alone. Jest me an' the baby. Patsy's no help. I'm so worried about li'l Rhonda not havin' her daddy aroun' fer a strong male role model. Her li'l tummy's jest wrecked, I know it an' with Momma bein' sick the way she's been, well... Poor Ed.

ED. They found the car, didn't they?

LYNETTE. Huh? Yeah. In a ditch off the highway near that Mister Softee. But I guess you know that... Poor Ed.

ED. I shoulda burnt it. Leave her nothin'.

LYNETTE. Ferget it, Ed. Whyn't you lay down. Cool off.

ED. I'm gonna make her sorry. I'm gonna make her pay. She'll be sorry she ever looked at that mush-mouthed scumbag. Damn! It's hot in here!

> *(The baby cries.)*

LYNETTE. Shhh! See now, there she goes! I tole you, Ed. Thanks.

ED. I'm gettin' outta here.

LYNETTE. Wait. Where you gonna go? It's pitch-black out. *(Crying gets louder.)* Ed, it's the middle of the night...

> (**LYNETTE** *exits to the baby.*)

ED. You never saw me, okay?

> (**ED** *takes a gun from his jacket pocket, lifts it to his eyeline, spins the cartridge, and takes aim. He then runs out the door as the baby continues screaming. Fade out.*)

Scene Two

(Later. The trailer. No light. The low howling of a dog or two. We hear a key fumbled in the door as **PATSY** *enters. She wears a full skirt with a ruffled top and gingham design.* **B.D.**, *dressed in a Wrangler-style cowboy shirt, jeans, and boots follows, stumbling up the steps.)*

PATSY. Oops, watch yerself. That first step is the big one. A light'd help. *(She flicks on the light.)* Welcome to the Mansion on the Hill.

B.D. Where's your restroom?

PATSY. Right thru there.

(He dashes off. Her eyes follow him.)

Do fries come with that shake? *(She sits, then half to herself.)* Damn. I lost my lowers. My eyelashes. *(She fusses with her hair.)* Whoo-doggy, that was some jamboree, wat'n it? You sure are a good dancer. Jukin' must be in yer blood.

B.D. *(Re-enters.)* Haven't danced like that since I was a teenager. Felt kinda rusty.

PATSY. Well, you didn't look a bit rusty to me, no siree. *(Beat.)* Oh boy, my head is spinnin' like a top.

B.D. You okay?

PATSY. I'm fine. Jest one two-steps too many. I needa wet my whistle. Want another beer?

B.D. No thanks, I'm a cheap drunk. Three's my limit.

PATSY. Wish I could say the same... Them flamin' hot wings sure didn't set too well. *(Beat.)* What a night! All these goin's-on. I jest hope Mavis don't have to let out that dress too much... Damn them curly fries.

B.D. You'll look great.

PATSY. God love ya fer a liar.

> *(She moves to the fridge, pulls out a beer, and pops it open.)*

B.D. This is a nice place. Everything's so...close. That's too bad about your house, though. How long you been in here?

PATSY. A month 'er so. We was in a motel fer a few weeks right after... Soon as Ed's workin' we're gonna get us a bigger place. On the ground. *(Beat.)* Oblah-dee, oblah-dah, it'n that what they say. "Life goes on."

B.D. Patsy, what d'you think happened to Ed? Where do you think he went?

PATSY. Truth is, I'm tryin' not to think about it. Ed 'n' J.B... I'd like to knock 'em both to kingdom come. Runnin' aroun' the middle of the night like a pair a' fools. Runnin' aroun' the middle of the night's somethin' to do, huh? That J.B. – blind when he's drunk an' blind when he's sober: "All them places look alike in the dark"! ...I get home an' see that black, smoky pile of what used to be, I swear my whole life jest passed before my eyes...an' I can't say that it interested me too much... Yeah, I sure know what "used to be" looks like.

> *(There is a sudden tapping sound on the window.)*

B.D. What's that knocking?

PATSY. Huh? Maybe it's the wind 'er a raccoon 'er somethin'.

> *(She goes to the window.)*

B.D. Who's there?

PATSY. Nothin'. I don't see anythin'. Maybe it's the trees.

B.D. We were gettin' some mean looks there tonight, Patsy. I think people're talkin'.

PATSY. Let 'em talk. They can talk till their tongues fall out fer all I care. Ignorant people got no room to talk. *(Beat.)* Ed is jest tryin' to prove somethin'. He's jest tryin' to be a big man.

B.D. He's been gone more than a week. The entire sheriff's department is out there looking.

PATSY. Yeah...both of 'em. You don't know Ed. I know Ed. He jest can't stand not bein' the center of attention. Don't worry, he'll be back. Besides, we got a play to do.

B.D. A play.

PATSY. The day after tomorrow. I jest can't hardly wait! Aren't you excited? Oh, yer jes an ole pro, it's nothin' to you. My horoscope today said, "It's a bumpy road with the moon in Cancer but yer fortunes improve with time."

B.D. "Fortunes improve with time," huh?

PATSY. Yep. That's what it said.

B.D. My dad. He'd love you.

PATSY. What? What about him?

B.D. He kept this big jar on a shelf in the basement full of fortunes from Chinese cookies. From the only Chinese restaurant in East Texas and the only restaurant we ever ate out in. Every Thursday like clockwork. *(Beat.)* I think it reminded him of the war. He loved the war – all his buddies and such... I think that was the only time he was happy... He's gone.

PATSY. Oh. I'm sorry.

B.D. I don't know where he went. He sure got outta here... Haven't seen him since. I was ten. After he left I used to come home every day from school, take that

jar down from the shelf, dump those fortunes on the
rug an' just look at 'em. There musta been hundreds.
I looked on maps and in bus station windows. On
trains that went past along the highway – but he was
never there. Then one day on the six o'clock news, I
saw him. It was a special bulletin about a tornado in
Port Arthur that had come and gone in five minutes
but "left devastation in its wake." People were crying,
holding babies and walking on their houses. And there
was my dad, hosting with a microphone. I called the
station and told them that my father had a son and to
come home right away. I told them I was sure. They
hung up twice. So, the next day after school, I took a
bus downtown to KLIF-TV and told them I was there
to see my father. They asked me questions and gave me
an ice cream cone. Finally, I saw him coming down the
hall. I was happy but he looked mad... The next day we
were both on the front page of the paper. I was "Rookie
Newsman's Love Child." *(Beat.)* He wasn't my dad
though and I got grounded with no TV for a month...
Funny thing is, he was just some guy – and now I don't
even remember his name...

PATSY. I'm sure yer daddy misses you an' I know he'd be
real proud a' you, too.

B.D. I never told that to anybody before.

PATSY. An' you tole me.

B.D. Patsy, I think I gotta get going. I think it's time for me
to go.

PATSY. Whaddaya mean? Why're you goin'?

B.D. I'm late. I'd like to stay –

PATSY. Then stay.

B.D. It's late. It's time for me to go –

PATSY. Let's get some music on. Keep this party goin'!
Yessiree!

(She goes to the counter, turns on the portable radio, and scrambles the dial looking for a song, creating loud static noise. After a moment, she pulls **B.D.** *to her and sings over the radio.)*

PATSY. "Buffalo gals won't ya come out tonight, come out tonight, come out tonight –"

B.D. I'm goin'!

PATSY. "And dance by the light of the moon."

B.D. I'm leavin' Patsy!

(He goes to the radio and turns it off.)

This isn't the right thing. It's not right.

PATSY. Well, tell me what it is Mister "Right."

B.D. Patsy, I like the play. I like being with you. I – I – care for you a lot. You're very sweet and you make me laugh. But you're married and I'm on my way out. Outta here. Outta this place. I been tryin' my whole life to leave.

PATSY. Me, too. I know.

B.D. Let me finish. I am *so* tired of Texas. I've been trying my whole life to leave. Last year, after Momma died I came back – again, closed up the house and that was that. I been spinnin' my tires ever since but it's time to go.

PATSY. We're so much alike –

B.D. We're nothing alike.

PATSY. I wanna get out, too. You know I do. There's nothin' here fer me anymore, either.

B.D. You got Ed. And my time is up. *(Beat.)* No, Patsy... I got a child somewhere – a son and his mother, somewhere – Dallas, I think, and I was never confirmed, my name isn't Arthur – that's from *Camelot* and I don't know French besides what you could read in a dictionary.

PATSY. You got a child.

> *(She slowly sits.)*

B.D. I have to do what's right. For once. I don't want to hurt anybody.

PATSY. Yer lyin'. "Dallas."

B.D. Here. Look. Wanna see?

> *(He takes out his wallet, pulls out a small, worn photo and, kneeling, hands it to her. She closes her eyes and slaps it out of his hand.)*

PATSY. I don't believe you.

> *(He picks it up, holds it to her face.)*

B.D. Look, Patsy. Look.

PATSY. No.

B.D. Look! See, Patsy.

> *(After a beat, **PATSY** slowly opens her eyes.)*

PATSY. He looks like you. He has yer eyes.

B.D. I have been laying awake at night thinking how this ever happened. How I coulda made such a big, big mistake –

PATSY. "Everythin's big in Texas."

B.D. I'm sorry about Ed.

PATSY. Don't talk to me about Ed. If he was here he'd take yer head off an' I can't say as I'd stop him. Ed's not a phony an' a fake.

B.D. If I ever thought anything more than a play would happen, I never –

PATSY. Could you not talk anymore?

B.D. You made me feel something after years of not stopping long enough to know if I ever could again. I'll always thank you for that. *(Beat.)* Be happy for me.

PATSY. Gimme a minute... *(Long beat.)* Well, Mister Bobby Don Flowers, I wish you all the best, I really do. "The show must go on," right? I hope you find yer family wherever they are. Yer son needs a father. That's the best thing you can ever be... When you get there, drop me a postcard. Sign it with a name only the two of us know – a sorta code – an' when *I'm* tired a' Texas, I can think about you in that car on the other side a' the road, stoppin' fer me in my dreams.

> *(**B.D.** takes her hand, kisses it, and walks out of the trailer, pulling the door behind him. A low howling in the distance. Fade out.)*

Scene Three

(The next evening. After midnight. A clearing in the woods outside town. **DUKE** *appears, walking slowly. He carries a bucket of chicken.)*

DUKE. Ed? Ed? I know yer here... This is yer spot. The secret spot. The spot nobody knows about. This is where yer old childhood treehouse used to be. You tole me all about it, Ed. This is where you come back to. So, jest come on out an' get yer chicken. *(He sets the bucket down.)* I brought this here chicken...

Ed, yer a missin' person. Yer picture's in the paper an' they 'nounced yer name on the news. Even in Waco. Yer well-known. I think you must be hungry...

So, come on out an' get it. *(He picks out a piece and starts to eat.)* I tole you I'm not a good spy. I said I shouldn't do it. I'm a bad spy. I like bein' in the play, though. An' I don't play an animal... MMMMMmmmmmmMM! I'm eatin' it all! ...I'm tryin' to help you out do what's right... I'M TELLIN' 'EM WHERE YOU ARE an' they're gonna come pull you outta them bushes an' accuse you of false disappearance! Now you really gone an' done it, hoooo-boy! They'll put you in jail an' then you'll wish you had this chicken!

(He takes one last bite and listens to the rustling of the trees as the lights fade.)

Scene Four

(Music up: "Down in The Valley."*)

(The theater. Lights up on the stage set during the opening night performance. The full view is a night sky with a painted full moon and cardboard trees. Fog from dry ice blows onstage. There is more distant howling. **PATSY** *runs on and goes into an awkwardly stylized ritual mime-dance indicating intense, almost hysterical joy. After a moment,* **B.D.** *chases onstage, pulling her to the floor. They kiss as he slowly lifts her in his arms to exit – then a loud thunderclap and flash of light as* **DUKE** *jumps out directly in their path from behind a tree.)*

DUKE. "Witch boy! Moonlight's a comin'. It's a comin'!"

B.D. "Leave me be."

DUKE. "You be lonesome..."

> *(***DUKE*** *goes into an elaborate "witch dance," incorporating all sorts of karate and jazz-type movements with lots of bouncing and slithering. There is chanting offstage in unison with* **DUKE**.*)*

"Hang yer head low, hang yer head low.

Down in the valley feel the wind blow..."

> *(***PATSY*** *"awakens" in* **B.D.**'*s arms.)*

PATSY. "John, John..."

B.D. "O Conjur man! Why?"

---

*Licensees will need to use a public domain recording of "Down in The Valley."

DUKE. "Take her away! Take her away!"

B.D. "Please! Spare my Barbara's life!"

DUKE. "We jest bringin' you back. Back to da moonlight wid us!"

B.D. "Please let me be human – jest a little while longer..."

(**PATSY** *has a "revelation.")*

PATSY. "You witches, ain't you?"

(**DUKE***'s "acting" becomes more intense as he points a stern finger at* **PATSY***.)*

DUKE. "She be married to someone else. Heed my warnin', witch boy!"

B.D. "I don't want yer warnin'!"

DUKE. "We won the life a' Barbara Allen. Back to da moonlight – an us!"

(Suddenly, there is a commotion down the center aisle as **ED** *appears at the back of the theater covered in leaves and mud. He pulls the gun.)*

PATSY. Oh my god! Ed!

DUKE. Ed!

B.D. Shit!

PATSY. Ed Tyson, drop that gun!

*(***ED** *races up the aisle toward the stage. Blackout. Gunshot.)*

Scene Five

(**LYNETTE** *at her kitchen table, on the phone,*
surrounded by newspapers.)

LYNETTE. She's a celebrity! Oh Momma, I wish you coulda
seen it. My baby in the papers!

She's a heroine. (*She speaks louder.*)

I said we're in the papers! I'll send you all the clippin's.
(*She reads.*) "TINY TOT SLIPS UP MADMAN!" "OH
BABY! SHE SAVES THE DAY!" I tell you Momma, it
was somethin'. He comes racin' up that aisle like he's on
fire. (*Beat.*)

Ed! Oh Momma – I never seen nothin' like it. It was
somethin'. We're sittin' there watchin' the play, it's right
near the end an' everythin's very dramatic, and them
chairs – well, you know my back, so I'm sittin' there,
I try to be on the aisle in case I gotta powder my nose
real fast an' li'l Rhonda's on the floor – she likes to play
with her Cootie Bugs – she's jest as quiet as a mouse
but she made a li'l wee-wee. All of a sudden there's a
commotion an' I look back and everybody's lookin' an'
Ed's got a gun. (*Beat.*)

A gun! An' he looks like a wild man – he was jes'
carryin' *on*, screamin' an' shoutin' at Patsy an' them
onstage. "Get away from my wife! I'll blow you to the
moon!" I feared fer my life! Then he comes racin' up
that aisle like he's on fire! – An' I gotta grab the baby or
he's gonna run right over her. (*Beat.*)

He's gonna squish her if I don't pull her outta the way!
An' then he slips there, all of a sudden he goes flyin' in
the air.

(*Beat.*) *He slipped on her pee-pee puddle.* It wasn't much
but it was enough, I guess. An' he goes flyin' in the air
an' that gun goes off. I never seen a thing like it – shoots

right through the simulated glass "Peaceable Kingdom" skylight they had put in at the center. Expensive, too. I worked them bake sales. *(Beat.)*

He shot through the roof! (Beat.)

Uh-huh. Then he lands right smack down on his backside – an' he's jest layin' there moanin' – I felt fer him. Then some a' the men jump on him an' they grab that gun an' jest take him away to the sheriff. *(Beat.)*

He's out now. He goes before the judge next week. *(Beat.)*

Mommy, I been thinkin' I might come up fer awhile – A week 'er so...fer a visit. An' I'll bring the little star. She misses her meemaw, the sweet thing. *(Beat.)*

Yer grandchild. When it happened we had all the papers here. We had all the reporters here an' let me say: they-were-impressed. I'm takin' her up to Woodville fer pictures. She's very photogenic.

(Blackout.)

Scene Six

(One week later. The local bus station. **DUKE**
*is sitting, two small suitcases at his feet. He
is eating from a bag of chips. He stares up at
the [unseen] TV mounted on the wall above,
which is playing cartoons [with sound].**
After a moment,* **B.D.** *enters, carrying a larger
suitcase with a duffel bag slung over his
shoulder.)*

DUKE. Got yer ticket?

B.D. Yep. Thanks for helping me down here, Duke.

DUKE. Yer welcome. I like gettin' up early like this. They
got good cartoons in the mornin' here – an' snack
machines.

B.D. You don't have to stay if you don't want, Duke.

DUKE. I want to, I don't mind. *(Beat.)* I'm sorry about the
play an' all... Too bad they closed it down without even
finishin' openin' night.

B.D. "Que sera sera..."

*(***DUKE*** stares blankly at him.)*

That's how it goes...

DUKE. I really liked doin' it though. Even with everythin'
happenin'. It beats bein' a goat.

B.D. Well, Duke, I'm sure there'll be another one soon.
Howard might be doin' *Midsummer Night's Dream*
next. He can use the same set.

DUKE. I don't know that one.

---

*A license to produce *Moonlight Sinatra* does not include a performance
license for any third-party or copyrighted recordings or images.
Licensees must acquire rights for any copyrighted recordings or images
or create their own.

B.D. It's by Shakespeare... It's about some people who love each other and get very confused.

DUKE. Sounds funny... Boy, it's gettin' hot. Summer soon.

B.D. *(Stretches out with a sigh...)* "Oh, that this too, too solid flesh would melt, thaw and resolve itself into a dew..."

> *(**DUKE** gives him a blank look, then pulls on his own hot, sticky shirt.)*

DUKE. Me, too... *(He stares at **B.D.**'s belt.)* That's some buckle you got there. It's great.

B.D. You want it?

DUKE. What?

B.D. I'll give it to you. For helping me.

DUKE. But that's a special one. It's got them masks. It's yers.

B.D. Well, I'm retirin' it.

DUKE. But you need it to hold yer pants up.

B.D. We'll trade.

DUKE. I'm not wearin' one...

> *(**B.D.** unbuckles and removes the belt. **DUKE** is agitated at this possibly shocking public display.)*

B.D. Well, now you are.

> *(He hands the belt to **DUKE**, who holds it up religiously, flashing the buckle in the light.)*

DUKE. Well, lookee there. That sure is somethin'...

B.D. I see it.

DUKE. *(After a beat.)* So, yer goin' up to Dallas.

B.D. You ever been to Dallas?

DUKE. Nu-uh... Ed's momma was up there 'fore she died. He's been there. *(Beat.)* Don't pay him no mind. He's nothin'. He ain't my friend no more. He's a jerk... So, yer gonna be on the radio. "B.D. the D.J."

B.D. Well, I gotta try out. It's my uncle's show up there: "Sunrise Sabbatical." It's an inspirational program.

DUKE. Momma likes them shows.

B.D. Yeah. And my family's up there, too. My son.

DUKE. I didn't know you had a son. How old is he?

B.D. Nine... No, eight. I haven't seen him in a while.

DUKE. Well, it's good yer goin' then. *(Another awkward beat.)* You wanna candy bar 'er somethin'?

B.D. No thanks. Duke, you could take off. The bus'll be here any minute.

DUKE. Yeah okay, I guess I'll go. I gotta give Momma her shot anyway. Patsy showed me how. I'm pretty good at it now but Momma still don't like it. Okay. Well. Thanks. I'll see ya. Take it easy. I'll listen fer you.

> (**DUKE** *walks off.*)

B.D. See ya...

> (*He waits for a minute, then the loudspeaker announces: "Seven a.m. bus from Houston to Dallas now arriving, Gate Three," then he stands and gathers his bags as the lights fade.*)

Scene Seven

(Late afternoon. **PATSY** *and* **ED** *in the car.* **PATSY** *is driving.* **ED** *sits in the passenger seat, scowling. He wears a neck brace.)*

PATSY. Why? Why on God's green earth, Ed? *(Beat.)* How was yer group?

ED. I don't like it.

PATSY. You don't gotta like it. You jest gotta go. "Don't like it." You got no choice. *(Beat.)* Why Ed? Why'd you pull somethin' like that? *(No response.)* You know what you coulda done? *(No response.)* We gotta see that counselor tomorrow. We better be ready fer that judge. Where'd you get that gun, anyway? I ast you.

ED. A box a' Cracker Jack. I tole you. From a guy.

PATSY. You never said who. I wanna know.

(She pulls over and stops.)

I wanna know. Who?

ED. Roy Hubbard. Okay?

PATSY. Roy Hubbard. Mister Mini-Golf himself. Roy Hubbard won't give you the time a' day. Roy Hubbard won't give you a job an' now he's givin' you guns?

ED. *A gun. One gun.* An' I bought it.

PATSY. You bought it alright.

ED. Gimme a break. I could trot over to the Quik Mart and have me a gun in two shakes, easy as pie. *(Beat.)* Don't you think I know what I done? Don't you think know? Boy, do I *know*. Why don't you think about what *you* done? Why don't you jest think about that?

PATSY. What *I* done? I run off, disappear an' come back swingin' a gun?

ED. You *know* what you did.

PATSY. *That* is in yer mind.

ED. He was in yer head.

PATSY. An' yer outta yers. I didn't do nothin'.

ED. Duke saw y'all. Everybody seen y'all. You turned yer back on me an' denied yer vows.

PATSY. I never turned my back on you.

ED. You *lie*.

PATSY. Nothin' ever happened. Nothin'. Duke should go tell stories at the Bookmobile. Nothin' ever happened with me an' Bobby Don... *Nothin'*...

ED. I think I better go ask him. That's what I think I better do.

PATSY. I think you done enough. I think you better think about un-doin' some things. Jest keep goin' to yer group an' keep...goin'.

ED. I don't wanta group. *(Beat.)* It's always me. What about what *you* do? We never hear another word about that. What about the Korean?

PATSY. Go diggin' that up. Ancient history.

ED. It don't matter. We was goin' together. You didn't even ask me.

PATSY. Ask you? He paid me three-thousand dollars jest to marry him. To get in the country. He was an alien.

ED. You took money fer it. What does that make *you*?

PATSY. I gave that money to Momma an' Daddy. Fer their trip.

ED. I don't remember where they went exactly... I seem to recall they went nowhere.

PATSY. Momma got sick. Damn you, Ed.

ED. Shit happens, okay Patsy? An' Bobby Don Flowers ain't no saint. Yer not. Me neither.

PATSY. That's fer sure.

ED. Gimme a break.

PATSY. YOU GIVE ME A BREAK! I had it fer the last time! I been embarrassed by you fer the last time. Everybody there that night. You ruined it. You ruined it all! I'll give you a break alright!

> *(She gets out and starts repeatedly slamming the car door.)*

ED. Quit that! People're lookin'.

PATSY. Let 'em look! YOU CAN TAKE THIS DAMN CAR AN' THIS PLACE AN' YOU CAN EAT MY DUST!

> *(**ED** gets out of the car, and they are shouting at each other.)*

ED. I'm sicka this shit. I wanta dog. I'm gettin' a dog.

PATSY. A dog?! That's what's on yer mind? A dog! Who's gonna take care of a dog?! No way, buster! Not me!

ED. I'M GOIN' TO PUP 'N' SUDS AN' I'M GETTIN' A HOT DOG! Jeez!

PATSY. I wanta a divorce. I swear I do. I'm the crazy one. Tell that to yer group.

> *(**ED** runs over and starts shaking her.)*

ED. You jest don't listen to me, that's yer problem. I don't wanta group. I want you.

> *(She starts pounding on him. He holds her tight.)*

PATSY. Damn you. Damn you.

*(Her punches slow; she collapses in his arms
and begins to whimper as he strokes her hair.)*

ED. Go ahead, baby. You ain't hurtin' me. *(Long beat.)*
Maybe we oughta get a dog... Remember Cha-Cha,
that ugly Pekinese yer momma had? I was so afraid a'
that dog. When I'd come over to the house to pick you
up, that dog'd always be there with his face pushed up
against the screen door. Made him look even uglier.
Remember? That Cha-Cha'd jump up an' always try
to bite me. I'd turn aroun' an' there he'd be. Droolin'.
Lickin' his chops. I hated that dog. Yer momma loved
him though so I hadda act nice. I always felt sorta
stupid, bein' afraid of that ugly little dog. It was hard
not to kick him. Had a set a' teeth... Shit...

PATSY. I hated him, too.

ED. You did? I always thought you loved him.

PATSY. I thought *you* loved him.

ED. I was jest actin'.

PATSY. He was a mangy mutt.

ED. Then he got hit by a car.

PATSY. No. He ran under that fire truck. Chasin' it. Momma
was crazy fer that dog... Ed, promise me.

ED. What?

PATSY. You gotta promise me. Do everythin' like yer supposed
to. Settle down. Do right.

ED. I was gonna ask you the same thing.

PATSY. Keep goin' to yer group.

ED. Stay away from yers.

PATSY. I don't think that director, Howard ever liked me.
Nobody good's left anyways... Ed, promise me.

ED. I'll keep goin', yeah.

PATSY. Nobody got hurt, Ed. Nobody got hurt.

ED. Let's hope that judge agrees. You wanna Coke 'er somethin'? Dr. Pepper? *(Beat.)* You okay?

(He starts to bark and nuzzle her.)

PATSY. Jest go on an' get it, Cha-Cha man.

*(**ED** exits, after a moment **PATSY** gets back in the car, turns on the radio, switches the dial, then turns it off. She closes her eyes and sits. She studies herself in the rearview mirror, then opens her purse, takes out a scarf and sunglasses, puts the scarf and sunglasses on. She steps out of the car and, leaning against the door, slams it, pushes herself off, and starts to walk away – then we hear **ED**'s voice.)*

ED. *(Offstage.)* Patsy! Hey, Patsy!

PATSY. Ed...

*(**ED** walks on, carrying a take-out tray.)*

ED. Where you goin'?

PATSY. *(After a beat.)* I'm goin'...to the fillin' station. To freshen up. It's so hot today an' I need to freshen up.

ED. Oh. Well, I got yer drink here. They was outta fries. Can you believe that? Outta fries. Shit. Somebody screwed up. Now what?

PATSY. What?

ED. Well, I thought you needed to freshen up? You better move it. I got bowlin' tonight...

PATSY. Yeah...

*(**PATSY** walks off. Fade out.)*

End of Play

PROPERTY PLOT

ACT I
PRESET:
Portable radio (stage right)
Telephones (stage right/stage left)
Beer cans (stage right)
TV remote control (stage right)
Box of cereal (stage right)

Empty chips bag (Ed)
Key ring w/keys (Ed)
Purse (Patsy)
Large carry-all bag (Patsy)
Bottle of nail polish (Patsy)
Bag lunch w/snack cake, banana and apple (Duke)
Comb and scissors (Patsy)

ACT II
PRESET:
Baby bottle w/milk (stage left)
Beer (stage right)

Small axe (Lynette)
Newspapers (Lynette)
Take-out bucket of chicken (Duke)
2 small suitcases (Duke)
Bag of chips (Duke)
Large suitcase (B.D.)
Duffel bag (B.D.)
Take-out tray w/bag and sodas (Ed)
(Hand)gun (Ed)

Note on the stage set: Due to space limitations of the original production, many scenes were suggested by a change in lighting and furniture pieces, e.g. two chairs for the rehearsal scene later used for the bus station scene. The car was suggested by a fabricated facade with two seats, doors, and steering wheel on casters rolled on and offstage as needed.